WHEN I GET BIGGER

BY MERCER MAYER

A GOLDEN BOOK • NEW YORK

Golden Books Publishing Company, Inc., New York, New York 10106

When I get bigger
I'll be able to do
lots of things.

I'll go to the corner store by myself...

I'll wait until the light is green.
Then I'll look both ways for cars
before I cross the street.

I'll have my own watch and I'll tell everyone what time it is.

I'll go on a bus to Grandma and Grandpa's.

When I get bigger I'll have
a real leather football...

...my own radio, and a pair of
superpro roller skates.

I'll have a two-wheeler and a paper route.
I'll make lots of money.

At the playground
I'll help the little kids
on the swings.

I'll make a phone call
and dial it myself.

I'll order something from a catalog…

…and it will come in the mail.

When I get bigger I'll camp out in the backyard all night long.

Or I'll stay up to
see the end of the
late movie.
Even if I get sleepy,
I won't go to bed.

But right now I have to go to bed...

…because Mom and Dad say…

...I'm not bigger yet.